W9-BGD-328

President Plump promised a wall

President Plump lost in the fall

All of Plump's Russians

And angry white men

Couldn't get Donald elected again

The President's Penis: A Member Remembers

A Memoir

By Pebis Plump

Dedicated to the Resistance

And the Forty-Five people who read the entire Mueller Report

An Introduction

By

Samuel Shyster
Literary Agent

Recently I was sent a manuscript by an agent of an unnamed government agency purporting to be the exclusive memoir of Donald John Plump's penis, which I thought initially, should be titled "A Member Remembers." But I digress...

To say that I was skeptical of the content is an understatement, but the night the manila envelope arrived and subsequently ten minutes thereafter I was met by the agent who, before he introduced himself, scanned my office for electronic listening devices. Finding none, he explained that he delivered the manuscript in paper form because the Russians hacked all White House emails.

The agent swore to me that the president's penis, which is an asset in so many ways, was activated for duty after the president secret conversation with Vladimir Putin in Helsinki, Finland. This occurred during the president's annual prostate examination at Walter Reed Hospital which was after the meeting with the Russian President. An agent, posing as a urologist, was able to insert a tiny microchip into Donald's Dong while inserting a small video probe into the First Penis. If this had not been a matter of National Security the probe would have never been inserted. What was discovered was a total surprise to the agent and his agency was that the President often thought with his penis in lieu of his brain. Many women have theorized that such was the case with all men, but until the agent, acting as urologist, sent the probe up the presidential penis there had never been a confirmation of that feminine suspicion. However, we can honestly claim that the President, at least, is one man who often thinks with his little head. Since the president has millions of followers there are no doubt other men who think with their dinky.

The president's prick is a patriotic penis and willingly communicated with the unnamed agency and provided great deal of information as well as his own personal memoir. I was offered the redacted version of the memoir to represent and what you are about to read is the actual report of Pebis Plump, the president's penis. There have been many tell-all stories and behind the scenes books about the Plump administration, but there has never, until now, been a book written by a source that is so close to the president. A source that has been with President Plump every day of his life.

In fact it was Mr. Plump who nicknamed his own penis while he was enrolled in New York Military Academy as it was something the boys there liked to do. I will let Pebis himself explain the origin in his name in his Forward, which he suggested we refer to more appropriately as Foreskin.

As a man gets older his sausage often fails to perform and the man feels let down. It is only a small step from erectile dysfunction to outright betrayal and while Watergate had John Dean none of Mr. Plump's advisors has had the courage to speak out against the president…until his penis.

Foreskin

My name is Pebis and I am the president's penis. Contrary to what Stormy Daniels has said, I am not shaped like a mushroom although I admit I have seen better days and I now get around with a pretty constant limp. I mean in my glory days, I once was a divining rod pointing to pussy from across a crowded room, like the night Eppy and I cavorted with all those beautiful models at Mar-a-Largo. Priapism was ascending that night. Priapus, you may be unaware, was a Greek god, the offspring of Dionysius and Aphrodite. He was a god of fertility and male genitalia and went around the ancient world with a giant wand, so to speak. Priapus hated donkeys which is kind of surprising because there are a great many jackasses in the world who worship their baloney pony.

Forget that nonsense about a boy and his dog. The true love is a boy and his wang. Ever watch how a two-year-old boy holds onto his wiener? It is if he is deathly afraid someone may dismember his member and he might wind up as, horror of horrors, a girl. That is how Donny and I became so close...Donny really held onto me tightly back then as if he could sense our destiny together as a future love machine.

During the 2016 Presidential Campaign there was quite a fuss about the Access Hollywood tapes that recorded Donny talking about "grab them by the pussy" because he was a big star and all. Well, the first pussy he ever grabbed was a four-year old wetback, the daughter of one o daddy's maids.

Fred Plump would never have a nigger maid, mind you, that was even worse than a nigger tenant (he was awfully fond of the "N" word) in one of his apartments, but he was not averse to a wetback maid or nanny. Anyway, little Donny pulled down the title girl's panties and was a tad shocked to see that she had a "hoohaa" and was missing a wing ding; so, curious, he moved his hand in to investigate and wound up grabbing his first pussy, but I can't recall the girl's name. Probably Maria, I would guess because the Mexicans are nuts about the Virgin Mary, Donny likes to say, that is when they aren't out raping people and smuggling drugs.

Now Donny says that is a bullshit story for you that is for sure, that Virgin Mary nonsense; although Donny has never told the evangelicals he doesn't believe in the Virgin

Birth. He is honestly amazed that the Evangelicals think he is a Christian. So he gives them a conservative judge now and then to keep them happy; it is akin to throwing a steak to a religious Rottweiler. Donny does not like dogs though. I think it is because dogs can sniff out bullshitters. And one thing Donny has always been all of his life is a consummate bullshitter. He puts the art into con artist. I mean is there a bigger con in the history of the con then fooling the entire nation and becoming president? Why he would want to run for a second term is beyond me. What does behave to prove? He pulled off the greatest con of all time. Of course, if he loses he and I will be headed for some hard time in prison. I really think his slogan for 2020 should be "Second Term or Prison Term: Your Choice America." But I guess that slogan is a bit too long for hats, huh?

How did I become "Pebis"? Why not Peter or Johnson or Excalibur? Well, when Donny was a cadet at the military academy all the boys were naming each other's members. One guy's wiener was called Dick Tracy which everyone thought was pretty lame. So, when we arrived at the school, I hadn't fully developed and the boys nicknamed me "Pebis," and that moniker has followed me to this day.

Even as a boy Donny was thinking presidential as he was inspired by Teddy Roosevelt, although I would have preferred Rough Rider to Pebis as a moniker.

Chapter 1
Plump Family Military Heroes

I thought I should begin with the history of military service in the family Plump as it is the shortest chapter in my memoir. Not exactly Grant's *Memoirs* or Caesar in Gaul.

Simply put, in four generations of Plump males not one of the Plump men has ever entered military service. You see there is a genetic yellow streak in Plump genes that affects not only the hair on their head but their spines was well. And it started with Friedrich, the President's grandfather, who emigrated from Germany at the age of sixteen. However, Friedrich like all other German males was obligated to serve in the military but he blew it off. Instead he headed to the gold rush in Alaska and opened a brothel where he mined the miners who paid in gold nuggets for the ah…services…Friedrich provided. He then sent the nuggets to his sister in New York City and she used the nuggets to buy real estate. So it can be honestly said that the Plump real estate empire owes its beginnings to pussy. Long before the Plump men were grabbing pussy they were exploiting it while all the time being pussies themselves.

Well, Friedrich fell in love and married a good German girl in Kallstadt when he returned for a visit in 1901. Her name was Elizabeth and the couple went to the USA until Elizabeth became homesick and begged to return to Germany and settle there. But the German government said "nein" and Friedrich and Frau were sent packing by a royal decree, a result of Friedrich's failure to do his military duty. There is no evidence that Friedrich's father provided a doctor for his son to claim that Friedrich had bone spurs and so Friedrich and his bride were banished to the United States of America. How different history might be had the Kaiser allowed Friedrich to repatriate.

The President's father, Fred Plump, was born in 1903, a sweet spot for military conscription in the 20th century. He was too young to serve in World War 1 and too old to be drafted in World War II.

Much has been made of the President as a shirker during the Vietnam War. I recall the day he received his draft noticed. Do I ever! I remember shrinking up like a spider on a hot stove. I think it was the smallest I have ever been since we entered puberty. Even Tommy and Teddy, our testicles, retreated into a prepubescence position before distention and our colon emptied its contents, unfortunately into our pants. Finally, after five deferments, we were about to face the music of John Philip Sousa, until Daddy intervened and found a compliant doctor to diagnose the future President with bone spurs. So, while other lesser men, like niggers and dumb crackers, were sent to the paddy fields of Southeast Asia, we were safe to continue our search for the perfect pussy. I certainly got a workout, let me tell you. Those were the as.\. Poontang on parade! Those years shaped me, both figuratively and literally, as I developed something of a previously mentioned mushroom head. I repeat: Not as bad Stormy Daniels made ii out to be. The President was in earnest when he stated that avoiding venereal disease was "My personal Vietnam...It is pretty dangerous out there. I feel like a very brave soldier."

Of course I was his point man, so to speak, and if anyone was going to get the clap it would be me. And we entered the bush like a grunt in 'Nam; we never knew what we would find? Herpes? Syph? I played a lot of Just-in Beaver back then.

And when the President grabs the standard on stage and literarily wraps himself in the flag, I admit to being erect. I mean, as the First Penis, I believe I should be patriotically standing at attention and the fact that the media does not notice my erect posture is due to the presidential girth which of course was a sign of affluence and health among Germans when Friedrich was a boy back in the Fatherland.

Today, of course, with a volunteer army. Don Junior and Eric have no need for a "doctored' diagnoses from an unscrupulous physician. So, no Plump has ever served in the military and that goes back over one hundred years. Cowardice does not just run in the Plump family, it canters.

Chapter 2
Our Childhood

Donny was not always the size and shape of a walrus. He was not always as roly-poly as his surname implies. I mean you don't really believe that he only weighs 239 pounds do you? Remember that Navy Doctor who claimed that was Donny's true weight? He became the big guy's pick to head the VA until they found out the guy had a little problem with the sauce. Donny's true weight is closer to 300 squishy pounds and he is the fattest president since Taft. Thank God the bathtubs in the White House are bigger than when William got stuck in one.

Donny's obesity bothers me. His rolls of blubber make me look smaller. If he would just lose fifty or sixty pounds I wouldn't seem so tiny. I mean, when he stands at a urinal and is about to pee he has to roll back layers of lard to even find me to tinkle. But there was a time...

When Donny was slim and trim, muscular and athletic. In the period I call B.S...Before spurs, as in bone spurs.

Even in elementary school, however, Donny was something of a bully. During the 2016 campaign he told a reporter, "When I look at myself in the first grade and I look at myself now, I'm basically the same. The temperament is not that much different."

Yes, he told the nation he was essentially a six-year-old and people still voted for him. I guess that was how much the evangelicals hated Hillary. Funny too, because for years Bill and Hill were Donny's pals. Donny gave big bucks to their political campaigns and Chelsea and Ivanka were BFFs.

In elementary school Donny was a little shit, a Dennis the Menace, and every teacher was Mr. Wilson. He even hit one mentor when he was in second grade. His music teacher. Donny's hair was a blond, not orange, pompadour and he was the center of attention on the playground and in the classroom. He was disruptive in class and a regular in detention. He developed his haughty surly look back then and he was never wrong. Donny's incorrigible behavior would lead to Daddy shipping him off to military school at age 13. That was where rich spoiled brats were sent back then, to military boarding school. From age 13 to 18 Donny learned discipline. And I seemed to live in a jockstrap in pre-pussy-grabbing puberty.

Actually, in elementary school Donny was the biggest kid and best athlete. And although Fred Plump was notoriously parsimonious, Daddy bought Donny the newest and fastest bike in the neighborhood. And by this time the Plump's had moved into a 23 room house with two Cadillacs in the driveway and a chauffeur and a cook. Fred Plump was a self-made man. Donny would never be. He received a few hundred million from Daddy, although he claimed it was only one million: one of the few times in his life when Donny downplayed rather than exaggerated.

Donny told the *Washington Post* that his parents thought the military academy's discipline would be a good influence on their son. "I was rambunctious" Donny admitted, in another rare truthful admonition. "I was a wise guy and they wanted to get me in line. Thinking back it was a pretty positive influence."

I have always thought Donny's military school discipline served him well through the trials and tribulations of his three marriages, his two divorces, and his numerous bankruptcies. I mean even those things were better than latrine duty and cleaning toilets with a toothbrush.

The fact that so many people think Donny is a great businessman really tickles not only me but Tommy and Teddy as well. We have chuckled about that often. I mean how many business guys can run a gambling casino in the ground? The house always win, except if the house is the Plump Taj Mahal. You have never heard anything until you have heard a testicle titter. Laughter from the loins is memorable indeed.

Now I know I am a purple helmeted love warrior, but Fred Plump was a prick...in the figurative sense. He wore a coat and tie around the house as if he was Dr. Real Estate and was always on call to show a property. He was a Goldwater supporter in 1964 and was a true conservative Republican. Mommy and Daddy did not allow their children to swear or, in the case of the girls, to wear lipstick. On the other hand the family had one of the first color television sets. Of course there were only a few shows in color and then the color was kind of runny, but no other family had a color TV. The losers!

Donny did well in military school. I, unfortunately, often suffered from jock itch. He was the best hitter on the baseball team and became the captain of A Company as a senior. Fred Plump could have sent Donny to any college after military school, but Donny chose a local college, Fordham University, so he could stay home and also work for his father. Suck up.

Chapter 3
Big Brother is Watching

Every family has a black sheep and in the Plump Family it was Fred Jr. The second oldest of the five Plump siblings Fred Jr., the first boy, was the family namesake and was expected to join father Fred in the family business. The only problem was that Fred Jr. did not want to be a real estate mogul; he wanted to be a pilot for TWA, something which was contrary to his father's wishes. Fred made Junior apply to the Wharton School of Business at Penn, but he was turned down and went to Lehigh University, where he thrived.

After Lehigh Fred harassed Junior to join the business and Donny joined in badgering his older brother to get with the program and join the firm. Fred Jr. continued to pursue a career as a pilot with TWA and his father mocked Fred Jr. for wanting to become a "chauffeur in the sky." Fred Jr. began to drink. Then he began to guzzle. He felt trapped and had no desire to enter the family business, but his drinking led to his washout from Trans World Airlines flight training and he was forced to take a job with the family business. His guzzling increased and he was diagnosed as an alcoholic.

Donny spoke to the *Washington Post* about his older brother and Fred Jr.'s alcoholism. He has often said that his brother's addiction was the reason he never drank. He was afraid the alcoholism might be genetic. Donny didn't tell the *Post* reporters that the night before the telephone interview that Fred Jr. had come to Donny in a dream. It was something akin to the ghosts visiting Scrooge on Christmas Eve from Charles Dickens' *A Christmas Carol.* In this case, the ghost of brother past.

A fresh-faced movie-star handsome Fred Jr. appeared in the president's White House bedroom. He smiled -he always had such pleasing smile- everyone always liked him, unlike Donny. I mean I love Donny, but that love is in my vested interest: we are attached to each other. We will take our connection to the grave or transgender surgery.

"Well now, Donny, I must admit I am impressed with you," Freddy said. "You have bullshitted your way into the White House."

"What do you want, Freddy?"

"I always knew you were a shit, Donny, but what you did to my son Fred Plump III was about as low as you can get, although I think it explains why you can put little brown children in cages."

"What are you talking about?"

"Cutting Fred III out of my share of dad's estate, especially when he had a child with cerebral palsy."

"We settled that."

"Yes, but he had to sue you"

"Yeah, and when he sued us we said why should we give him medical care?"

"How about because the boy was your great nephew, jag off?"

"Hell, I said we settled it... Hey Fred III was getting 200 grand a year for doing nothing for the company."

"But you got Dad to change his will."

"Hey you were dead, you loser. So what?"

"So I am gonna to haunt you."

"Sticks and stones will break my bones but haunts will never hurt me."

"You know you are going to hell, don't you?"

"Whatever. I can make a deal with the devil. I made a deal with Kim. I also did a deal with Roy Cohn; he's got to be working down there. He'll put in a word for me. You read *Art of the Deal* didn't you? Maybe I should send a few copies to wherever you are...I could autograph them for you."

What was it that Mark Twain said about heaven and hell? You went to heaven for the climate and hell for the company? Donny would always need an audience even if it was an audience of lost souls. Like the ones at his rallies. Empty heads were one thing, but empty seats were worse. And you thought Donny didn't read books? He doesn't. My agent at the agency-which-shall-not -be- named sends me audio books and I listened to a Twain book being read by the Hal Holbrook while Donny sat mesmerized watching *Fox and Friends* and tweeting to his 64 million followers on Twitter. But I digress. Back to the dream…

And so help me in the dream Donny laughed and Fred Jr withdrew. In the morning Donny dismissed the dream about Fred Jr, to a case of indigestion from eating too many Big Macs. Fred Jr. returned to haunt Donny the next night only to be met by Donny saying, "I am glad no one ever tried to get you help for your alcoholism. When you died you cleared the way for me."

Fred Jr. shook his head in disbelief at his younger brother and said with a hint of regret in his voice, "I even had my friend at Penn interview you for transfer to the Wharton School from Fordham."

"Nice guys finish last, that's what Leo Durocher said, Freddy…"

(Donny knew his baseball, which is one thing he knew, that and how to avoid paying income taxes.)

…"And you just prove Leo's point. You never understood that people are expendable, Freddy. When they are no value to you, cut them out of your life and let them go...even if they are relatives. Now get lost. I have some Muslims to ban in the morning and some wetback families to break up and I need my beauty sleep."

Donny had always resented Freddy, as Fred Jr. was commonly known. Freddy was better looking, Freddy was nice, everybody loved Freddy. Freddy could be trusted. If only Daddy and Donny hadn't hounded Freddy to join the family business, Freddy might have had a long, healthy life, I think. But there was one thing I would not permit. Donny may be a little shot on conscious but his dick isn't: Donny once thought that he should piss on Freddy's grave and one night we visited All Faiths Cemetery in Queens and a zipper came down and this trout was out of his trousers, but I let him down. I was obstinate. I would not make water and after a moment of struggle I was returned to our pants. On all subsequent visits to Freddy's grave we have been accompanied by other family members, all of whom are genuinely sad at Freddy's passing.

Chapter 4
Conspiracist-in-Chief

Perhaps because one of Donny's best buds was David Pecker of the *National Enquirer* and Pecker was the master of "Catch and Kill" journalism and the purveyor of cover-ups and conspiracies dating back to the alien cover-up at Roswell, New Mexico seventy years ago, Donny loved conspiracies almost as much as a quarter pounder with cheese.. And sometimes he started his own. Conspiracies that is. How about the time he said Ted Cruz's pappy was involved in the JFK assassination, that Ted's daddy was pals with Lee Harvey Oswald. Wasn't that a hoot? And even after Donny slurred his father's name, Rafael (Ted's real name) is always ready to pucker up and kiss the First Buttocks of the United States.

Then Donny spread the theory that Supreme Court Justice Scalia was murdered. And, of course the Clintons were involved in Jeffrey Epstein's death. Somehow. Bill probably taught him how to tie a hangman's knot, I guess. Maybe since Hillary was a witch she just flew into Epstein's cell on her broomstick and put a spell on him to off himself. I don't know; Donny never clarified how the Clintons whacked Jeffrey. He is always a little light on details for his conspiracies.

And, of course the Clintons killed Vince Foster too. Remember him? Of course you don't. Nobody does. That conspiracy is colder than Foster's corpse. Foster Grant? Yes. Vince Foster? No. Shades yes. Shade no.

But let's go over some of Donny's Greatest Hits, the conspiracies. That he, the President of the United States, has helped to spread. The Conspiracist-in-Chief.

Tops, of course, is the lie that Barack Obama was not born in the United States. And its corollary, Obama is a Muslim. Donny is a Birther. A "Birther" is a white racist Republican who says Obama was never born in the United States and was therefore not a legitimate president. I mean how to explain that a black man was elected president (twice!)in a nation with a white majority? That a black man was the only Democrat since FDR to receive a majority of votes twice in a presidential election! Obama even released his birth certificate showing he was born in Hawaii in 1961. Donny didn't give up that lie until late in the 2016 campaign. Funny thing is Donny had been a liberal New York Democrat. He backed Democratic candidates, albeit white ones. Of course there are still some white people in the U.S. that believe Obama is a Muslim even though he was a member of the United Church of Christ, not the United Church of Islam.

Vaccines cause autism. Donny was outed as saying that vaccines caused autism. If science contradicts Donny's gut, he ignores it. He goes with his gut instinct. And why not? His gut is pretty massive. It is bigger than his great brain.

Hence, windmills cause cancer. Well, I guess that explains *The Man of La Mancha* maybe, huh? No wonder Quixote was tilting at the windmills! He was fighting cancer! Still love the music, though.

Muslims are attempting to put in sharia law into the U.S.: this one has resonance with evangelicals who have been behind the laws banning abortions because that is what they believe. They want everyone to bend to their beliefs. Kind of like ISIS with a cross instead of a crescent. Don't mess with the existing Theocracy. Have an abortion and we will burn you at the stake! Suffer not a bitch to live…or something like that.

Three to five million illegal votes were cast in the 2016 election, but none for Plump, which is why Hillary beat Donny in the popular vote. That really galls Donny that he lost the popular vote. He likes to piss on her photograph by the way.

Obama wiretapped Plump Tower. Donny is obsessed with Obama and has never forgiven Barack for humiliating him at the White House Correspondents' Dinner back in 2011, but that is the subject of an entire chapter. But what really frosts Donny's cake is the possibility that New York City will rename a few blocks of Fifth Avenue, the street on which Plump Tower rests, as, horror of horrors, Barack Obama Avenue. That would be an excellent example of urban trolling, I admit, but then what does Donny have to complain about; he only owns two floors of Plump Tower anyway. Other specious claims…

Global Warming is a hoax perpetrated by the Chinese. But I especially like…

It might not be Donny's voice on the Access Hollywood Tapes. And a gorilla does not shit in the jungle either, right?

I can almost guarantee that before this book goes to print Donny will have retweeted a new conspiracy or three. You can count on it. It is certain as death and taxes and a Melanie face lift.

Chapter 5

Bromances and Reminiscences

I remember getting erect when Donny met Vladdy at that Moscow beauty pageant, Miss Milky Way Galaxy or whatever it was. Just kidding, it was bigger than that, it was Miss Universe and yet there was not even one non-human entrant. What about Miss Vulcan or Miss Romulan or Miss Klingon? Miss Tribble would have been nice.

On June 18, 2013 Donny tweeted: "Do you think Putin will be going to the Miss Universe Pageant in November in Moscow- of so, will he become my new best friend?"

Well the answer to that question is pretty obvious and it is why I am writing this book. After the pageant, Donny said, "I was in Moscow a couple months ago, I own the Miss Universe pageant, and they treated me so great "(including Miss Congeniality performing a golden shower I might add). "Putin even sent me a present, beautiful present with a beautiful note. I spoke to all of his people. And you know, you look at what he's doing with Obama. He's like toying with him. Toying with him." Donny, I admit, is fixated about Obama. I think in Donny's mind Obama is a black Freddy, a guy everybody likes. Donny, on the other hand, likes Putin.

Of course late in the campaign Donny said he didn't know who Putin was. You don't know how hard that was for Donny to deny Putin. Why I guess, my evangelical friends that it was as hard for Donny to deny Vladimir as it was for Peter to deny Jesus. But he and Vladdy had a hearty laugh about it when they met in Helsinki with no Americans present. Donny thanked Vladdy for the election help and apologized to him for saying he didn't know him during the height of the campaign and Vladdy had smiled, with a slight little KGB case officer Kompromat smile at Donny and reminded Donny of the pee-pee tape, Donny's money laundering and other shady business details and how Donny would never want any of that to come out to the public and it wouldn't if sanctions were lifted and remained lifted. Heck, if he was a good boy the Russian troll farm would be up for an encore of election interference in 2020. Putin even had Kompromat on Mitch McConnell, information worthy of his nickname "Moscow Mitch": a Russian aluminum plant for his home state of Kentucky as at thank you gift for Moscow Mitch's help in lifting the sanctions against Mother Russia. Shucks, Putin reminded Donny that the Russians had even given money to the N.R.A. and the GOP.

In essence, in Helsinki, Donny became Vladdy's bitch. I half expected Putin to give us a jar of Vaseline as a going-away present, I really did… Putin even dangled the Plump Tower Moscow in Donny's face; it was the ultimate Muscovite mirage. Have you never asked yourself why has Donny been so consistent with regard to Russia when he has flip-flopped on everything else? Nyet? Well there is a simple explanation: The Ruskies have the Kompromat on him, that is why.

But President Putin isn't the only world leader that has been the subject of a Donny bromance. Donny loved Canada Prime Minister Trudeau' s magazine cover pic, cutting the cover , writing "Looking Good!" and sending the cover to the Canadian Embassy. …Things have cooled since then, but what might have been…Oh Canada!!!!

Donny also has dreams about him and Kim Jong Un, there was one dream where they are dancing naked together like two happy happy hippos on the borderline between North and South Korea, crossing and re-crossing the border together as cameras clicked again and again. But his most often repeated dream is Vladdy on his horse, bare-chested... In the dream Putin is tying up his horse to a hitching post outside the Plump Tower Moscow and I am as stiff as a leftover ICBM, my mushroom about to lose its cap in anticipation. You see, my friends, Melania is a trophy wife and the First Couple hasn't had coitus since Barron was born, because Donny does not like f**king mothers. You can call him a racist, an unhinged sociopath, a moron or a nefarious prevaricator, but you cannot call Donny a Motherf**ker. He just isn't. I remember that night when we conceived Barron. Let me just say that my performance that night was a sprint and not a marathon and after the Lady M learned about the Stormy Weather, so to speak, there were no clouds up in the sky or space between her thighs, and the welcome mat was withdrawn forever. I mean really, do you think a beautiful woman like Melanie would like making love to an orange walrus? I mean Donny is even missing tusks and a mustache and resembles more manatee than walrus, come to think of it. She already had all his money and had given him a son. Too bad, too, I always enjoyed the few times I was allowed to visit her vagina. It was the Versailles of vaginas, and believe me I have been in many women's "homes."

Poor Lady M, Donny had promised her he would lose the election, and now here she was trying to be a white version of Michelle Obama, like she was some kind of white chocolate, I guess. I mean Lady M even stole Michelle's speeches, remember? Of course Lady M is the first Flotus to wind up on porn pages. I wonder if those evangelical preachers that support Donny have seen Lady M in her birthday suit. It is a top of the line outfit, that's for sure. She has the kind of body that Michelangelo might have sculpted if he wasn't a homosexual.

I wonder if Pat Robertson ever drooled over those "graven images" of FLOTUS being naughty. Or do they just excuse her bawdiness by reminding all disbelievers that Eve was naked as well? I mean do we really know what Eve *really* had going with the snake? There was no *Garden of Eden Enquirer* back then to tell us. I mean if the first woman in the Bible had a chance to model she might have done porn as well. If that isn't in the Bible it should be. Be Best! Show us your hairy nest!

But in the years before Lady M and the hormonal changes of puberty when Donny became interested in sex, he always had to be the top dog, among the small fry. He once said that he is the same person he was back in first grade and that he hasn't changed at all. He isn't known for telling the truth, but on this subject he actually did.

Grab them by the pussy...he sexually assaulted a fellow nursery school girlfriend...he started early...I mean we did not know what was up when we were three-years-old I think it was merely curiosity then as he had no idea why girls didn't have little wangs.

Father Fred, on the other hand, had an enormous one-eyed willy. Daddy's dong was a schwanzstucker, a really big schlong. I think Donald was always jealous of daddy's dick. And when one is a little boy a father's penis seems huge.

At military school the boys participated in a "bird pull," where other boys would first measure their members with a ruler and then pull each other's wieners. Donny often referred to the bird pulls as Oscar Meyers… If I have any appearance of a mushroom head it is-probably from my days as a cadet and all of the Oscar Meyers I was involved in. I mean how could Donny admit to that to avoid the Army? To the casual observer such behavior might have been deemed homosexual. So much easier to make up a whopper about bone spurs with the help of one of Daddy's tenants who was also a doctor. Donny had one friend who had paid a Park Avenue shrink $500 to say the guy was a fag to avoid the draft. But Donny would never want to be unfit for service because of homosexuality. That kind of stuff could follow a guy around, Donny thought. And of course Donny secretly feared that he might be a latent Hershey highwayman, as he sometimes referred to sodomites, as evangelicals might say. Hey, back then homophobia was accepted, what can I say? Donny still refers to gay men as fags. And he does not mean British cigarettes.

I still get an erection whenever Donny thinks of his MAKE AMERICA GREAT AGAIN hats. I mean Hitler had his brown shirts, but Donny has his red hats, even if they are made in China, like Ivanka's purses. Maybe that was why Donny used to keep a copy of *Mein Kampf by* his bedside. That is what the media reported. That is fake news! That is a lie; the actual book was *My New Order*, a book of Hitler's speeches. Now do the campaign rallies make more sense? Right out of Adolf's playbook. Let us take you back to the thrilling days of yesteryear, hi ho, Nuremberg away!

Chapter 6

The Making of the President 2016

Theodore White made nice living writing books about presidential elections. Some pundits say White changed how journalists have followed politics ever since 1960. White started with *The Making of the President 1960* which detailed the election of John Fitzgerald Kennedy. White went on to write subsequent “Making of” books. But had Theodore White written about 2016 his opening chapter might have been set at the 2011 White House Correspondents Dinner in Washington D.C. where Donald John Plump was the subject of ridicule by the then President Obama.

Well, pundits have written that humiliating evening was the start of the Plump Campaign. But Donny had thought about running years before as a candidate of the Reform Party. Other pundits have mentioned this and dismiss the pundits that say the 2011 event was the catalyst. And Donny later dismissed any correlation, but I can tell you that he wasn't happy, that he was infuriated and it took all his discipline to not stand up and shout at Obama. He was seething. But, of course, Obama was only giving Donny payback for the birther nonsense. Yet the birther business, believe it or not, made Donny a player, not in the Stevie Nicks' lyric sense because he had always been a player in the bedroom, but in the political sense because it created a group of followers, a core of crazies that are his true believers, Donny's base today. I mean Donny can act like the Anti-Christ and evangelicals are blind to it, as if they never read the *Book Of Mathew.* Probably too busy listening to the sermons of Joel Osteen, the televangelist who zooms around in a Ferrari. But back to the dinner…

Donny received an invitation to the 2011 White House Correspondents Dinner from his present-day nemesis, the *Washington Post.* Plump was not only the leader of the Birther Movement, but he was a reality TV star, the host of NBC's *Celebrity Apprentice*, which was a popular program. Donny was flattered to be invited and to be included with the movers and shakers of the nation. He never sensed the ambush.

Oh, he tried not to scowl, but he did purse his lips like he did when he was younger and a teacher called him out in class. I was proud he didn't flip off Obama. I mean Obama did a full five minutes of Plump jokes.

"No one is happier, no one is prouder to put the birth certificate matter to rest than the Donald," Obama began. "That's because he can finally get back to focus on the issues that matter, like; Did we fake the moon landing? What really happened in Roswell? And where are Biggie and Tupac?"

The president didn't stop there. "All kidding aside, obviously we all know about your credentials and breadth of experience. For example, no, seriously, just recently in an episode of *Celebrity Apprentice*, at the steakhouse, the men's cooking team did not impress the judges from Omaha Steaks. And there was a lot of blame to go around, but you, Mr. Plump, recognized that the real problem was a lack of leadership and so, ultimately, you didn't blame Little John or Meatloaf - you fired Gay Busey. And these are the kinds of decisions that would keep me up at night. Well Handled, sir. Well handled!"

Of course we learned the next day that during the Correspondents Dinner Seal Team Six had been dispatched to kill Osama Bin Laden, the architect of 9/11, making Donny look even more preposterous in comparison to President Obama. That fact made Donny seethe for days.

And then there was Seth Meyers, the comedian host of the Dinner, who went on insulting Donny longer than Obama. Said Meyers, "Gary Busey said recently that Donald Plump would make an excellent president. Of course, he said the same thing about an old, rusty bird cage I found…

"Donald Plump has been saying that he will run for president as a Republican - which is surprising, since I just assumed that he was running as a joke."

Well, Seth, the joke is on you and the other elitists who laughed at Donny that night. Donny got the last laugh after all. Donny is in the White House and the White House Correspondents Dinner is Event for the D list on C-Span, the network that is forever showing rooms filled with empty chairs...

In 2015 when Donny began his campaign for president Seth Meyers invited Donny to appear on his highly rated program, but Donny insisted that Meyer apologize for his 2011 jokes before Donny agreed to appear. It was Michael

Cohen ("I would take a bullet for Mr. Plump"), the family fixer who contacted the show with Donny's demands. An on-air apology no less. You don't think my man holds a grudge? Four years is nothing. If Dorothy Parker had been alive during Donny's reign she might have written "Women and Donald Plumps never forget." Plump might look like a manatee, but he was one manatee with a memory.

If you wonder which Meyers' joke got up under Donny's grill, it was, "Donald Plump often appears on Fox, which is ironic because a Fox on Donald Plump's head." That is the worst thing a comedian can do, make fun of The Donald's hair. He is fussier with his hair than a debutante is before she makes her coming out appearance. But what the heck, it is the best hair money can buy. 24 carat locks.

Chapter 7
Witch Hunting We Will Go

Witch hunting we will go
Witch hunting we will go
High-low the media
Witching hunting we will go.

Donny has often claimed that the "Russia thing" is a "witch hunt." If so, Robert Mueller sure busted up a few covens. More people have been indicted during the Plump Administration than any other presidential administration in U.S. history. Of course, the beauty of Donny's witch hunt claim is that the American people have not read the *Mueller*

Report. Neither have most members of Congress for that matter.

Agent X read the entire report to me. Basically it goes like this. Russia helped Donald John Plumb get elected. They messed around in all fifty states. They used Google and Facebook and more trolls than a library of fairy tale books to spread disinformation to a gullible public that believed all the bovine excrement uploaded to social media. Heck a Russian businessman even texted the previously mentioned Family Fixer (and now Jail Bird). Michael Cohen that he had stopped the "flow of tapes from Russia."

In an April, 2019 article in *Rolling Stone* wrote, "Buried in a footnote in Section II B of Volume II of the redacted *Mueller Report* is a single reference to supposed kompromat the Russian was rumored to have on the president - the infamous 'pee tape.'"

The media has since called the 'pee tape" the "pee pee tape", but Donny prefers to refer to it as the "Golden Shower Thing."

Anyway in the grand scheme of Russian election interference the "pee-pee Tape" is only a dribble of disinformation. You see, folks, Vlad wanted Donny to win so that Donny would remove sanctions against Russian oligarchs, like the rich Russian that rents Moscow Mitch.

As previously mentioned, Donny and Moscow Mitch worked together to take away penalties imposed by the Obama Administration for invading and taking over Crimea, which was part of Ukraine.

Heck, we knew about that tape in October 2016, a week or so before the election. Did the Russians influence the 2016? Does a Russian bear poop in Siberia?

The Russian helper who killed the tapes was Giorgi Rtskhiladze. The Golden Shower Thing was part of the Steele Dossier which has been discredited by right wing media. For what that is worth. Giorgi would also be the go-to guy on the Moscow Plump Tower project, Donny's impossible dream.

In Volume 2of *The Mueller Report,* the Special Counsel lists ten instances of possible Obstruction of Donald J. Plump. Since less than one-percent of Americans have actually read the report, I believe it is best that I go over them like a David Letterman "Top Ten" list.

#10 Conduct Involving FBI Director Comey and Michael Flynn. Michael Flynn? If you add and "O" to his surname it sounds like a cute little leprechaun. Flynn was a National Security Adviser to President Plump and Mike lied to the FBI about conversations he had with the Russians. These conversations were not about the Bolshoi

Ballet, Donny had Jimmy over for dinner and during the meal (Three piece KFC meals on Presidential china) the president asked Comey for "loyalty". Earlier in the day Donny had a meeting with Jimmy and asked Comey, "I hope you can see your way clear to letting this go, to letting Flynn go. He is a good guy. I hope you can let this go."

#9 "The President's reaction to the continuing Russia investigation."

Remember the Keebler elf that escaped Cookie Land and became our Attorney General. You can't? Here's a hint: Kate McKinnon played him on *Saturday Night Live.* Yes, I know she played a lot of Plump people…Jeff Sessions. We called him General Recusal. You see Donny asked White House Counsel Don McGahn to talk Jeff out of recusing himself on the Russia investigation. When McGahn didn't do it, Donny asked Jeffery directly. Then Donny called the CIA and NSA and asked them to "dispel the suggestion that the President had any connection to Russian election interference effort. He twice asked Comey to say that publicly.

#8"The President's Termination of Comey."

Since Jimmy wouldn't tell the world that Donny was not playing footsie with Vladdy, in May 2017 Donny canned Donny, but not to his face. Jimmy was in Los Angeles at the time. Donny told a little fib saying that he had fired Comey on the recommendation of the DOJ. That's hoot. Donny never listens to anyone; he does what he wants. And then like a lot of guys, he brags about. The *Mueller Report* stated, "The day after firing Comey, the president told Russian officials that he had 'faced great pressure because of Russia,' which had been 'taken off 'by Comey's firing.

#7 "The appointment of Special Counsel and efforts to remove him."

"Oh my God, this is the end of my presidency. I'm fucked," the president says forlornly on page 78 of Volume 1 of the *Mueller Report.* Nah! As long as the DOJ policy states you can't indict a sitting president and the U..S. Senate is stacked with Senators more afraid of Republican primary than the Almighty, Donny will survive any impeachment trial. In short, Donny tried repeatedly to have Robert Mueller shit-canned.

#6 "Efforts to curtail the Special Counsel's investigation."

Donny used Corey Lewandowski to deliver a dictated message to Attorney General Sessions. The message stated for Sessions to publicly say the Mueller investigation was "very unfair."

Corey did not work for the government so he gave the message to Rick Dearborn, a White House official, to deliver it to Sessions. Rick Dearborn did the right thing and sent the message to the circular file.

#5 "Efforts to prevent public disclosure of evidence."

As of this writing, Donny's stonewalling continues. That is the only wall that he seems to be building, a stonewall.

#4 "Further efforts to have the Attorney General take control of the investigation."

Donny is nothing if not persistent. He hounded General Recusal for months to take over the investigation from which he had recused himself.

#3 "Efforts to have McGahn deny that the President had ordered him to have the Special Counsel removed."

Donny instructed McGahn to get rid of Robert Mueller. The press got wind of this. Donny went more berserk than usual. He told White House officials to tell McGahn to rebut the press accounts. McGahn refused.

McGahn is off Donny's Christmas Card lit.

#2 'Conduct towards Flynn, Manafort, (Redacted.)

Hell, let me cut to the chase. Donny promised pardons to his capos. Clam up and walk out.

#1 "Conduct involving Michael Cohen."

Donny lavished Michael with praise when he remained loyal to the Corleone…ah Plump family until Michael turned on him. While Michael was obeying the code of silence, the Omerta, Donny dangled the pardons, but when Cohen flipped president Plump called him a "rat." Vito would understand.

Now the next time you are at a snobby elitist cocktail party and the people there are pretending that they have read the *Mueller Report* this chapter will serve you well and you will be better at pretend than everyone else. And honestly wasn't that what you wanted as a child, to be better at pretend than the other kids? Don't thank me, for that, just do me a favor; get someone else to buy this book.

We are going to need all the royalties we can get for legal bills after we leave office.

Chapter 8
Stupid Is as Stupid Says

You no doubt recall that Mrs. Gump often told her son that "stupid is as stupid does." Had Mrs. Gump lived long enough to witness the 2016 presidential campaign she might have changed her homily for Forrest to "stupid is as stupid says." And, it embarrasses me to say this, but Donny said some really stupid shit during the campaign…and since then. How can one man make a smart phone sound so dumb? Call it Twitter on the shitter. For many of Donny's early morning tweets are sent while he is straining at the stool. Unlike the King (Elvis) who died on the throne, Donny's middle name has often betrayed him when he has sat upon it, leaving Mr. President clogged. Yes, Donny is constipated quite often. And it is rather obvious that he is full of it.

Donny's political ascent began with his descent on a Plump Tower Golden Escalator (now a registered National Historical Site) and the speech that launched his campaign shortly thereafter. Who can forget the lofty rhetoric of his first address, the greatest oration since Abe elucidated at Gettysburg. No piddling "four score and seven years ago," for Donny. He got right to the point without all that literary la-de-da (what is a "score" anyway?)

"When Mexico sends its people, they're not sending their best. They're not sending you…(he kind of lost his train of thought here) They're bringing drugs. They're bringing crime. They're rapists. And some, I assume, are good people."

Considering the number of illegal immigrants that were working at Mar-a-Largo and Plump golf courses at this time his chutzpah really amused me as well as Tommy and Teddy the tittering testicles, and I almost had a golden shower of my own while he spoke. I did dribble a bit, but thank heaven for Depends. (this is not product placement)

Later in the same speech Donny added, "I will be the greatest Jobs president that God ever created. I tell you that…, and I'll...I would build a great wall, and nobody builds walls better than me, believe me, and I'll build them very inexpensively, I will build a great, great wall on our southern border. And I will have Mexico pay for the wall." In retrospect Donny's "Mexico will pay for the wall" may be his Bush 41 moment: "Read my lips, no new taxes." Anyway, Donny was off in the campaign.

About John McCain, Donny famously opined, “He was a war hero because he was captured. I like people that weren’t captured (or even went, I might add.”

In a CNN interview Donny claimed, “I cherish women. I want to help women. I am going to be able to do things for women that no other candidate would be able to do.” I might suggest that a change of article from “for” to “to” might be more honest. I mean no one, not even the womanizer JFK, has screwed more women, both literally and figuratively, than my Donny. Trust me, I was there. I was his enabler-in-chief.

Notable and quotable quotes from the campaign and after:

“I have a great temperament. My temperament is very good, very calm.”

“Everything I have done virtually has been a tremendous success.”

“I believe in clean air, immaculate air, but I don’t believe in climate change.”

“I know more about ISIS than the generals do.”

“I watched when the World Trade Center came tumbling down. And I watched in Jersey City, New Jersey, where thousands and thousands of people were cheering as the building was coming down. Thousands of Muslims were cheering."

"How stupid are the people in Iowa? How stupid are the people of the country to believe this crap?" Since Iowa voted for Donny in 2016, I guess the question is rhetorical,

"If you see somebody getting ready to throw a tomato, knock the crap out of 'em would you? Seriously. OK? Just knock the hell out of 'em. I promise you I will pay for the legal fees. I promise. I promise." This occurred at one of his campaign rallies. Not as often though as Michael the Black Man appeared holding his "Blacks for Plump" sign behind the podium. Was he paid? Were the Shell workers paid to show up? Fake news. Fake news! " Lamestream media!"

"I would bring back waterboarding. And I'd bring back a hell of a lot worse than waterboarding." This is a promise he has kept.

"Well just so you understand? I don't know anything about David Duke, OK? I don't know anything about what you're even talking about with white supremacy or white supremacists." That was then. David Duke and the Klan endorsed Donny for 2020.

In March 2016, when Donny was still pals with Joe and Mika, he said on *Morning Joe* when asked who his foreign policy consultants were, “I’m speaking with myself. Number one, because I have a really good brain and I’ve said a lot of things.” Hard to argue with the last part.

“Do I look like a president? How handsome am I, right? How handsome?” He asked the crowd at a rally in West Chester, Pa in April 2016.

On Cinco De Mayo 2016 Donny tweeted. Happy Cinco De Mayo! The best taco bowls are made at Plump Tower Grill. I love Hispanics!” (Just not Mexicans).

I am the king of debt. I understand debt better than probably anybody. I know how to deal with debt, so well. I love debt.” And he does, Donny brought his expertise in debt to our national debt. A couple trillion more!

He told CNBC on May 6, 2016, “I have borrowed, knowing that you can pay back with discounts. Now we’re in a different situation with the country. But I would borrow, knowing that the economy crashed, you could make a deal (is the Bald Eagle behind door number 1, 2 or 3?). And if the economy was good, it was good. So, therefore, you can’t lose.”

At a rally in California Donald spotted a black man and called out enthusiastically, ‘Look at my African-American here!” It was his Archimedes moment and the black guy was his Eureka. And it was not even Michael the Black Man. It was another guy!

In an interview with Bill O'Reilly (remember him?) in June 2016, Donny claimed, "I was the one that really broke the glass ceiling on behalf of women more than anybody in the construction industry, and my relationship, I think, is going to end up being very good with women."

And at a rally in Richmond in June 2016, Donny first said what he has often since repeated, ""I am the least racist person, the least racist person that you've ever seen, the least."

"I feel like a supermodel except, like, times 10 OK? It's true. I'm a supermodel."

"Russia, if you're listening (they were), I hope you are able to find the 30,000 emails that are missing."

Referring to Barack Obama at Florida rally in August 2016, Donny said, "He's the founder of ISIS. He is the founder of ISIS, OK?"

"Tiny children are not horses."

"Covfefe."

"Laziness is a trait in blacks."

"Environmentally friendly light bulbs can cause cancer."

"I could have prevented 9/11."

"I am the chosen one." He looked up at the sky when he said this. A comedian later quipped, "Praise the Lard." I know I shouldn't have laughed at the joke but Tommy and Teddy were tittering and I couldn't help myself; I dribbled a drop or two.

"I am a very stable genius."

"Any Jew that votes Democrat is disloyal." I guess that makes 79% of the Jewish voters who voted Democratic in 2018 traitors. Donny picked that trope up from *My New Order,* when Hitler called Jews disloyal to the state.

"The gun doesn't pull the trigger, a person does. And we have great mental illness." Donny said this after he received a phone call from the N.R.A. and reneged on a promise to expand background checks for guns-after the El Paso and Daytona massacres. In our defense, I must say that Donny is a fan of Waffle House Restaurants.

Donny has also begun to refer to himself in the third person…"Nobody has been tougher on Russia than Donald Plump," Nobody has more respect for women than Donald Plump," "China has total respect for Donald Plump's very, very large brain." And my personal favorite: "There has never been a president like Donald Plump." And you thought he never told the truth. Oh ye of little faith…read the next chapter.

Chapter 9
Evangelicals 'R Us

Televangelist Pat Robertson once told his audience he had a vision of Donald Plump seated "at the Right Hand of the Lord?" Where was Jesus? On a bathroom break? Working another galaxy? Hawking crucifixes on QVC?

So Pat thinks Donny is on the same level as Jesus Christ. That is pretty rare company. I mean everyone knows Donny is the King of Israel, but the King of Kings?

"God came to me in a dream last night," Reverend Robertson testified. "He showed me the future, He took me to heaven and I saw Donald Plump seated at the right hand of our Lord."

Since I go wherever Donny goes, I do not recall that happening. Have you ever noticed that Pat Robertson wears a good many wool suits? I remember when Donny and I were in Sunday school together and the preacher cited *Matthew* 7:15, "Beware of false-prophets, they come in sheep's clothing but inwardly they are ravening wolves." Heck, Jesus says the same thing again in *Mark*. Donny has always thought Pat Robertson was a wackadoodle, but

Donny thought Pat ran a great con. Two weeks after 9/11 Pat had the late Jerry Falwell on his program and together they blamed the attacks on gays and feminists because God was angry with America. I remember Donny laughing when he heard that. Look, Donny is not an atheist. He believes in God. He believes He just thinks he IS God (like Alec Baldwin in the movie *Malice).*

The evangelicals are a hoot; they should be called the evergullibles. They actually believe God chose Donald Plump President. They may have a point, because, well, the people didn't.

Robert Jeffress is the pastor of First Baptist (why is there never a Second?) Church in Dallas, a megachurch with over 12,000 members. He said that Donny made a better candidate than Jesus.

"You know I was debating an evangelical professor on NPR, and this professor said, 'Pastor, don't you want a candidate who embodies the teaching of Jesus and would-govern this country according to the principles found in the Sermon on the Mount?' I said, 'Heck no.' I would run from that candidate as far as possible, because the Sermon on the Mount was not given as a governing principle for this nation. When I am looking for someone who's going to deal with ISIS, I don't care about the candidate's tone or vocabulary, I want the meanest, roughest, son of a you know what I can find and believe me that's biblical."

I mentioned that Fred Plump was a Goldwater supporter in 1964 and Donny and I heard an interview with Senator Goldwater years later when he said, "Mark my word, if and when these preachers get control of the Republican Party, and they are surely trying to do so, it's going to be a terrible damn problem. Frankly these people frighten me. Politics and governing demand compromise. But these Christians believe they are acting in the name of God, so they can't and won't compromise. I know, I've tried to deal with them." RIP AuH20.

Donny keeps the holy-rollers happy by backing abortion restrictions and giving the Christian Right conservative judges in hope that SCOTUS will reverse Roe vs. Wade and put women back in their place, the place that the Hebrew patriarchs demanded. It is all about the patriarchy, the belief that "anatomy is destiny." Three steps behind girls.

And Donny has reframed Christ's beatitudes and the evangelicals have adopted Donny's version over the Lamb's. Let's take a look…

Jesus: "Love your enemies, do good to those who hate you, bless those who curse you."

Donny: "When people wrong you, go after those people, because it is a good feeling and because other people will see you doing it. I always get even."

Jesus: "Love your neighbor as yourself."

Donny: "I will build a great, great wall on our southern border and I will make Mexico pay for the wall."

Jesus: "I was hungry and you gave me something to eat. I was thirsty and you gave me something to drink. I was a stranger and you invited me in."

Donny: "I'm putting people on notice that are coming here from Syria as part of this mass migration, that if I win they're going back."

Jesus: "Those who exalt themselves will be humbled, and those who humble themselves will be exalted."

Donny: "Sorry losers and haters, but my I.Q. is one of the highest- and you all know it! Please don't feel so stupid or insecure; it's not your fault."

Jesus: "I have not come to call the righteous, but sinners to repentance."

Donny: "Why do I have to repent? Why do I have to ask forgiveness if I'm not making mistakes?"

Jesus: "Blessed are the merciful, for they shall be shown mercy."

Donny: "I fully think apologizing is a great thing. But you have to be wrong. I will absolutely apologize sometime in the hopefully distant future if I'm ever wrong."

Jesus: "Blessed are the peacemakers, for they will be called the children of God."

Donny: "I could stand in the middle of Fifth Avenue and shoot somebody and wouldn't lose voters."

Jesus: "Do not store up for yourselves treasures on earth...For where your treasure is; there your heart will be also."

Donny: "Part of the beauty of me is that I am very rich."

Jesus: "This is my body given for you; do this in remembrance of me."

Donny: "When I drink my little wine and have my little cracker, I guess that is a form of asking forgiveness."

So the evangelicals have chosen Donny over Jesus and xenophobia over the Good Samaritan. Even Pastor Franklin Graham, son of the famous evangelist Billy Graham, has proclaimed that Donny was chosen by God. And considering all the places Donny and I visited and all the adultery we committed and all the Commandments we've broken, it really is surprising to think we are holy. That we are "chosen."

Perhaps I will be honored as a religious symbol to accompany the Flour-De-Lis. Or a religious relic like the finger bone of Saint Rocco who was the patron saint of dogs until the Pope demoted him to a nonentity. The President's Penis, think of it; I am like a divine dildo. The penis for the Parousia which is the Greek word for the Second Coming. Think
Of the money Pat Robertson can make selling replicas of the President's Penis on the *700 Club. The Parousia Penis! BOGO! Our operators are at the phones! Call Now!*

After all, was it not Ralph Reed, founder of the Faith and Freedom Coalition, who said, "There has never been anyone who has defended us and who has fought for us, who we have loved more than Donald J. Plump?" Why should I not become a religious symbol for the religious right? My spirit has visited more females than the two Gabriel visited in the Bible (Mary and John the Baptist's Mom Elizabeth).

Franklin Graham as political as his father was apolitical, believed that Donny was being attacked by Democrats, Republicans, the media and even the Prince of Darkness himself. Franklin called for a special day of prayer on June 2, 2019 to protect President Plump from his enemies. Hosanna in the highest!

"We're on the edge of a precipice," Franklin warned. You could almost feel the Rapture approaching! "Time is short. We need to ask God to intervene. We need to ask God to protect, strengthen, encourage and guide the President."

Amen to that.

Chapter 10
Nasty Women

Many readers may be disappointed that I am not going into details of Donny's dillydallying. I am not one to bleep and tell. This is not a salacious memoir and there are too many lawsuits pending for me talk about either Plump's paramours or his prey as I might be named an accomplice. So rather than descend to the gutter, I will write about the strong women, the women that stand up to Donny and drive him batshit crazy: the nasty women.

Recently Donny referred to Mette Fredeiksen, the Prime Minister of Denmark as "nasty" for turning down Donny's offer to buy Greenland from the Danes. She had the temerity to call Donny's offer "absurd" and was labeled "nasty" for her trouble. Seriously, I thought Donny might purchase Lolita Island in lieu of Denmark now that Eppy offend himself. I mean we saw some good times on Lolita Island, let me tell you.

Helpfully, *Axios* made a list of women that Donny verbally attacked. *Axios* also reported that Donny thought up a great idea: use nuclear weapons to stop hurricanes. Nothing like the trade winds to spread some fallout from radiation. If the storm surge does not kill you, the radiation will. Donny gets some nutty ideas but sometimes he has Macadamia moments and nuking hurricanes was one of them. But back to nasty women...

While Mette showed her mettle, no woman gets under the First Skin more than Hillary Rodham Clinton. "If Hillary Clinton can't satisfy her husband what makes her think she can satisfy the country? She doesn't have the look, she doesn't have the stamina." And of course the chant at his campaign rallies from the loudmouth lemmings, "Lock Her Up!"

Then there is the super smart Elizabeth Warren: "Pocahontas is at it again! Goofy Elizabeth Warren, one of the least productive U.S. Senators, has a nasty mouth. Hope she is a V.P. choice."

Heidi Cruz (Rafael's wife): Donny tweeted side by side photos of Melanie Plump and an unflattering picture of Heidi with a caption: "The images are worth a thousand words." Once again the Senator from Texas (via Canada) did not defend a family member. JFK wrote a book about brave senators entitled *Profiles in Courage.* Do not expect Senator Cruz to be included in a sequel. I hear *The Yellow Rose of Texas* playing in my mind but the lyric has changed from Rose to Streak. *Oh the yellow streak of Texas we call him Teddy Cruz...*

Some of the other Nasty Women:

Justice Ruth Bader Ginsburg: "What does she weigh? Sixty pounds?"

Justice Sonia Sotomayer: "Her health. No good. Diabetes."

Mika Brzezinski: "I heard poorly rated *Morning Joe* speaks badly of me (don't watch anymore!) (He does) So how come low IQ Crazy Mika along with Psycho Joe came to Mar-a-Lago three nights in a row around New Year's Eve, and insisted on joining me. She was bleeding badly from a face lift. I said no."

Maureen Dowd: "Crazy Maureen Dowd, the wacky columnist for the *New York Times* pretends she knows me well - wrong!"

Megyn Kelly: "You could see there was blood coming out of her eyes. Blood coming out of her whatever." Donny also called her a "bimbo.

I recall the time Donny called a *Philadelphia Inquirer* reporter named Jenny Lin who was writing a story on Plumb businesses in Atlantic City. Unfortunately, Ms. Lin remembers too: "Then Mr. Plump began to yell at me. He told me I had shit for brains. He told me I worked for a shit newspaper and said what sort of shit was I writing. I was stunned. He hung up." But what *Axios* didn't mention was that Donny called Ms. Lin's editor and called Ms. Lin the most offensive term for a female in the English language. If you don't know the word, ask a woman, I won't use it.

Cher: "I don't wear a rug - it's mine. And I promise not to talk about your massive plastic surgeries that didn't work."

Angelina Jolie: "I really understand beauty. And I will tell you she's not. I do own Miss Universe. I do own Miss USA. I mean I own a lot of different things. I do understand beauty and she's not."

Columnist Gail Collins wrote that Donny called her a "dog and a liar with the face of a pig," after she published a column Donny didn't like.

I won't even get into the comments he made about Rosie O'Donnell. Too many, too often.

So in essence Donny loves women until they challenge him. Strong women are Donny's Kryptonite.

Chapter 11
The Campaign Rallies

The last book that Donny read cover to cover, besides *The Art of the Deal* was Adolf Hitler's *My New Order*, the book of the Nazi leader's speeches. Many in the media have been criticized by Plump supporters for comparing Donny to Adolf. But I am here to tell you the comparison is valid and his campaign rallies are great examples because they are designed just like those get-togethers of those fun-loving fascists in Nuremberg.

A rally is actually a play in three acts with each scene building to the arrival of the leader in act three. The leader must not be on time, the leader must let the crowd get into frenzy of anticipation. That is Storm Trooper Rally 101. Straight from *My New Order.*

When the first Mrs. Donald J. Plump sued for divorce, the nasty woman added to her filing how Donny read and studied Hitler's *My New Order,* underlining key passages. Donny was fascinated by the speeches' impact on the media and politics. To say that Donny learned a lot by studying Adolf's exercises in rhetoric is an understatement. Donny adopted quite a few of Adolf's techniques as well. At least Ivana didn't mention the armbands with the black spider or that Donny, who cannot recall the words to *God Bless America,* marched around their bedroom in his birthday suit singing perfectly every word of *Deutschland Uber Alles.* I was always at attention for that. The good old days! Perhaps it is understandable that Donny forgot the words to *God Bless America* since it was written by a Jew.

In an article the *New York Times* explained the campaign rallies as "Part presidential ego boost, part political organizing tool and part Wrestle-mania,' Make America Great Again" rallies are the defining event of the Plump era."

Well, yes, the *Times* is right as far as it goes, but they saw no connection of President Plump rallies to the Nazi wing dings of the 1930s. As I said, the rally is usually in three acts. Act 1 begins with a tweet from Donny several hours before the rally to excite the base. In Act 1, the supporters line up at the venue. Diehards have arrived the night before, many have driven hundreds of miles to attend and be in the presence of President Plump. Donny is a Rock Star! And like groupies they follow The Leader from rally to rally.

The people at the venues intermingle with each other, all true believers, coughing up another $25 for a red MAGA hat which are made in China. There is never a BOGO on our red hats! Sometimes, some in the audience are paid to be there by a pro-Plump employer. I have no choice. I have to go. I accompany Donny everywhere. But, at the rallies, I often listen to an audio book graciously provided to me by Agent X. I really enjoyed *Becoming.*

People at the rallies are selected for V.I.P. slots, these are the people who will stand behind Donny on stage. These are coveted positions. And if you don't cheer and smile, you are replaced.

In Act II, a campaign official comes out to excite the incoming crowd. Plump supporters take their places. A confession: we always try to overbook the venues to ensure all seats are filled and there is an overflow crowd to meet Donny when he arrives. It keeps him happy. A campaign rally is like a Big Mac and fries and an apple pie for Donny: comfort food. Sometimes it hits a KFC bucket level and Colonel Grease lubricates Donny's mood with his secret original recipe.. to rephrase Stephen Foster..."Campaign rallies sing this song, MAGA, MAGA, campaign rallies hours long, MAGA every day . Let's yell 'lock her up,' let's shout 'send them back," bet your ballot on Donald Plump, there's nothing more to say!!"

In *1984* George Orwell envisioned "two-minute hates." But the Englishman lacked the vision of Donald J. Plump. His rallies are two *hour* hates.

Local Republicans come on stage to bask in the lights. Shortly thereafter Donny arrives, walking slowly through the crowd like Jesus entering Jerusalem on Palm Sunday, but without the ass. Save the centaur jokes.

Act 111 begins with all the local Republican candidates genuflecting before the President. It sort of resembles the capos of the Corleone family waiting to kiss Michael's hand in *The Godfather.* After all the toads and sycophants are introduced, Donny takes over and begins to speak, invariably reliving the 2016 campaign, reminding one and all how the fake news media assured the world that Hillary would win.

"Remember, remember, they were expected to win. And there was no way that Donald Plump can get to 270. You know the Electoral College was set up so we can't win, except we had one problem: We won a lot of states that haven't been won for many years by Republicans. A lot of states. A lot of states."

And the crowd always cheers like fans at a stadium concert when Paul Mc Cartney sings *Hey Jude* for the zillionth time. For Donny, it is always about 2016. I am surprised Donny hasn't suggested that 2016 be named the Year 1, like the French Revolution calendar. Of course ours is a Reign of Error not Terror…so far

And Donny rambles on for an hour or two and then wishes everyone goodbye and departs, reinvigorated by his beloved base and dreaming of the comfort food that awaits him on Air Force One. Please, oh Lord, don't let the mashed potatoes be cold.

In retrospect I often wonder if Joseph Goebbels had had warm apple strudel ready for Adolf after a rally, perhaps Hitler might never have started WWII. It is something to think about; The calming effect of comfort food.

Chapter 12
It ain't Over Until the Fat Fella Tweets
(with apologies to Lawrence Berra)

Lawrence (aka Yogi) Berra was the Philosopher King in pinstripes. The Yankee catcher was as famous for his sayings as he was for his World Series rings. He once compered baseball to opera (or what he thought opera was) when he remarked, "it ain't over until the fat lady sings," meaning, in some way, that a baseball game was not complete until the final out. Now Yogi envisioned a large lung warbling soprano, wearing a Viking helmet with horns no doubt, and knocking out an aria at the end of the opera. Well, in a modern Yogism, it is the same for President Plumb. "It ain't over 'til the fat fella tweets."

To say that Donny is a Twitter Critter is an understatement. His tweets go out day and night. His tiny hands whimsically change foreign policy with a few misspelled words sent to the internet. A tariff tweet can rattle the stock market. He has made the word "smart" a misnomer in "smart phone." Yes, Donny is my guy but Twitter is his addiction. Freddy had alcohol, Donny has Twitter. And even though I Love Donny he can tweet some stupid shit.

There have been thousands of tweets from Donny over the years with "Worst Tweets" lists done annually. I decided to use 2018. If you are not sated by my choices, the Twitter-verse has all of them catalogued. If you are a masochist, have at it.

On 1/2/2018, Donny tweeted:

"North Korean leader Kim Jong Un just state that the 'Nuclear Button' in on his desk at all times.' Will someone from his depleted and food starved regime please him that I too have a Nuclear Button, but is much bigger & more powerful one than his, and my Button works."

I guess there is no bigger phallic symbol than an ICBM, but this manhood through megatons was pretty scary and Donny contemplated "fire and fury" until a Secret Service agent brought him two quarter pounders with cheese to calm him down.

Today, Donny talks fondly of love letters from Kim and it kind of reminds me of a formula rom-com when the girl and boy hate each other at the beginning but they fall in love in the third act. As I have mentioned before, today when Donny dreams of Kim they are dancing together like Fred and Ginger in need of Weight Watchers.

1/6/2018

"Now that the Russian collusion, after one year of intense study, has proven to be a total hoax on the American public, the Democrats and their lapdogs, the Fake News Mainstream Media, are taking out the old Ronald Reagan playbook and screaming mental stability and intelligence."

1/6/2018 (back-to-back tweets combined)

"Actually, throughout my life, my two greatest assets have been mental stability and being like, really smart. Crooked Hillary Clinton also played these cards very hard and, as everyone knows, went down in flames. I went from VERY successful businessman to top T.V. Star to President of the United States (on my first try). I think that would qualify me as not smart, but genius…and a very stable genius at that!"

The first thing I thought when I read that tweet was Mr. Ed, the talking horse, was a stable genius, too. Somedays I even identify with Wilbur. (You young folks can look the TV show up on YouTube.)

2/27/2018

"WITCH HUNT!"

Worse than Salem in 1692, let me tell you! I half-expected FBI agents to cut a pentagram into the White House lawn. That's how paranoid Donny was getting. But then f you knew what I know…

3/6/2008

"The new Fake News narrative is that there is CHAOS in the White House. Wrong! People will always come & go, and I want strong dialogue before making a final decision. I still have some people that I want to change (always seeking perfection). There is no Chaos, only great Energy."

The next time you are on a White House tour you will enter through a revolving door that Donny copied from one of hotels, It isn't for the tourists, but rather for the employees as the turnover rate is the highest in history.

4/6/2018

"President Xi and I will always be friends, no matter what happens with our dispute on trade. China will take down its Trade Barriers because it is the right thing to do. Taxes will become Reciprocal & a deal be made on Intellectual Property. Great future for both countries."

Don't believe what the economists say, consumer, you don't pay the tariff on Chinese goods, the Tooth Fairy does.

4/25/2018

Donny tweeted "MAGA" in response to a Kanye West tweet that has since been deleted..

I guess the African-American that Donny saw in his rally audience and was so excited about was Kanye after all.

5/29/2018

"Sorry, I've got to start focusing my energy on North Korea Nuclear, bad Trade Deals, VA Choice, the Economy, rebuilding the Military, and so much more, and not on the Rigged Russia Witch Hunt that should be investigating Clinton/Russia/FBI/Justice/Obama/Comey/Lynch etc."

And that is an incredible list to complete when you don't start your day until 11 am because of "Executive Time." No wonder Donny doesn't have time to read.

6/25/2018

"Congresswoman Maxine Walters, an extraordinarily low IQ person has become, together with Nancy Pelosi, the Face of the Democrat Party. She just called for harm to supporters, of which there are many, of the make America Great Again movement. Be careful what you wish for Max!"

Unfortunately for Donny when the Democrats won back the House Maxine became the Chairwoman of the House Financial Services Committee which recently subpoenaed Donny's tax returns. Maxine and Nancy could have been added to the Nasty Women chapter.

6/27/2018

"HOUSE REPUBLICANS SHOLD PASS THE STRONG BUT FAIR IMMIGRATION BILL, KNOWN AS GOODLATTE II, IN THEIR AFTERNOON VOTE TODAY, EVEN THOUGH THE DEMS WON'T LET IT PASS IN THE SENATE , PASSAGE WILL SHOW THAT WE WANT STRONG BORDERS & SECURITY WHILE TH DEMS WANT OPEN BORDERS= CRIME, WIN!"

Even though Donny used all caps to show this was an important tweet, calling on the Democrats to pass a bill in the House when they were in the minority was an impossibility. But our base does not know Civics, so what the hell. Republicans controlled both the House and Senate in 2018. If Moscow Mitch wanted the bill to pass, it would have.

7/3/2018

"After having written many best selling books, and somewhat priding myself on my ability to write, it should be noted that the Fake News constantly likes to pore over my tweets looking for a mistake. I capitalize certain words for emphasis, not b/c they should be capitalized."

Most voters don't realize what a great write Donny is. *The* Art of the Deal is far superior to JFK's *Why England Slept* or *Profiles in Courage.* And certainly *My Life and Struggle with Bone Spurs* eclipses Teddy Roosevelt's self-aggrandizing memoir *Rough Riders.* And Dwight Eisenhower's *Crusade in Europe* cannot hold a literary lamp to Donny's *Crippled America.* And, if you believe Donny wrote those books himself, I have a condo for sale at the Doral Country Club where Donny plans to hold the

2020 G-7 meeting. The Emoluments Clause of the Constitution does pertain to President Plump. It is all about the Benjamins for us.

8/3/2018

"Lebron James was just interviewed by the dumbest man on television, Don Lemon. He made Lebron look smart, which isn't easy to do. I like Mike!"

As in Michael Jordan, of course. Michael Jordan does not criticize Donny, Lebron does.

8/6/2018

"California wildfires are being magnified & made so much worse by the bad environmental laws which aren't allowing massive amounts of readily available water to be properly utilized. It is being diverted into the Pacific Ocean. Also must tree clear to stop fire from spreading."

Donny never acknowledged Climate Change might have something to do with the fires. Smokey the Bear came to Donny in a dream and Donny told Smokey what should be done. He told Smokey he knew more about forest fire management than the forest rangers…and Smokey. I thought Smokey was going to hit Donny with his shovel in the dream, but we woke up.

9/27/2018

'Judge Kavanaugh showed America exactly why I nominated him. His testimony was powerful, honest and riveting. Democrats' search and destroy strategy is disgraceful and the process has been a total sham and effort to delay, obstruct and resist. The Senate must vote."

I am reminded of the failed attempt by Nixon to put G. Harold Carswell on the U.S. Supreme Court. Nebraska Senator (R) Roman Hruska in defending Carswell said, "Even if he were mediocre there are a lot of mediocre judges and people. They are entitled to a little representation, aren't they?" Not in 1970, but in 2018? Senator Hruska was just ahead of his time. Mediocrity had its day with Kavanaugh.

10/16/2018

"Just spoke with the Crown Prince of Saudi Arabia who totally denied any knowledge of what took place in their Turkish Consulate. He was with Secretary of State Mike Pompeo."

Donny would be the first to admit that he never covered deals with Saudi sociopathic sovereigns in *The Art of the Deal.* Even when information about hit men and bone saws came out ,Donny was not going to give up a chance of a Plump Tower Mecca. Besides the dead guy worked for the *Washington Post* which is Fake News.

11/7/2018

"Tremendous success tonight! Thank you to all."

On Election Night 2018 Donny felt more comfortable with "alternative facts." The damn Dems picked up 40 seats in the House.

12/21/2018

"The Democrats are trying to belittle the concept of a Wall, calling it old fashioned. The fact is there is nothing else's that will work, and has been true for thousands of years. It is like the wheel, there is nothing better. I know tech better than anyone & technology."

I blame the lack of a completed wall on Moscow Mitch. For the first half of Donny's term the Republicans controlled the House and the Senate, but all they really wanted were conservative judges and a tax cut for rich folks. I still believe that Mexico will pay for the wall. And I also believe in Plump Tower Moscow. Sometimes I feel like little Natalie Wood in *Miracle on 34th Street* saying "I believe, I believe." For so many of us Donny is our Kris

Kringle. He has always been Santa Claus for Tommy, and Teddy and Me. We love him and we always will. This member will always remember Donald J. Plump.

There is no doubt that as I write this Donny will not be silent. His Twitter account has over 60 million followers. But then remember Pat Robertson saw Donny sitting at the Right hand of God. Considering this, you would think Donny should have a heck of a lot more followers.

Epilogue

Some readers may consider me a circumcised traitor for writing this memoir. But what man over sixty has not, at one time or another, been betrayed by his penis? Remember General Jack D. Ripper in *Dr. Strangelove* and his soliloquy about vital essence?

Yes, an older man can no longer count on his best friend, his wiener. Wasn't Washington's best friend Benedict Arnold? Wasn't Jesus's top disciple Judas? Did not both of those men betray their friends?

A penis is no different. A penis often betrays an old man. And Donald John Plump is old. He might read this memoir, but I doubt it and Fox News will never mention it, let alone review it, so it is doubtful that he will ever learn about my memoir. He doesn't read; he's like Chance the Gardener in *Being There;* he likes to watch.

The Never Ending Story

I thought we were finished this book until recently when Donny took a Sharpie to a weather map and so the book continues like the stupid Rambo saga.

When Ivanka was a little girl one of her favorite movie was *The Never-ending Story.* That's Donny; he is a never ending story and so I have decided that I will, from time to time, add another chapter or two to the memoir as we proceed toward the 2020 election.

Appendix A
King of the Jews

I am a fan of Randy Rainbow and recently on Facebook I watched Randy sing a parody of *Jesus Christ Superstar* which he dubbed *Cheeto Christ, Stupid Czar.* Randy's rendition was a reaction to Donny's early morning tweet of August 21, 2019, which itself was a retweet of radio host Wayne Allyn Root who proclaimed Donny "King of Israel" and the "second coming of God. Of course the Second Coming is supposed to be Jesus' gig, but what the hey. After all, if the Southern Baptists can have portraits of Christ as blond-haired, blue-eyed Aryan instead of a chocolate fella who speaks Aramaic instead of English, then why not a corpulent Christ, why not a Big Mac

Messiah. Isn't the Buddha fat? Why can't Christians have a dumpy deity as well?

Even though Mr. Root's roots as it were, are in Judaism, he is a convert to Christianity and theologically off-base. Jews, picky people that they are, do not recognize Jesus as God or the Messiah. A rabbi? Yes. An Essene? Surely. But the Son of God? Nah. Still waiting for Him.

Actually, all Root was doing was giving Donny a promotion. Pro-Plump Christians had been comparing Donny to King David, he of the Five Smooth Stones stuff and the Goliath rubout. The Good Book (and Leonard Cohen) says that David was a chosen by the Lord to lead the Israelites. And yeah, David had his own Stormy Daniels in Bathsheba, but unlike Donny he didn't pay upfront. So David was a sinner's sinner, but he was a divinely ordained sinner. So when Evangelicals are confronted with Donny's dirty deeds, his sexual assaults, his rapes, his obscenity and his seemingly endless prevarications that would even shame Pinocchio, he gets a pass from the holy people because he….is…white. Non-white saviors need not apply.

Now the problem is when comparing Donny to Jesus there is a tad of problem: Jesus is without sin. Donny has more sins than he has golf courses. Of course Roman emperors claimed themselves divine, so perhaps Donny thinks himself an emperor instead of president and so was quick to agree that he was "chosen."

Maybe Divine Right of Kings should be expanded to include presidents. However, according to the *Book of Mark* Jesus will return on the clouds and not on Air Force One.

And then there is another theological problem for conservatives. Christian tradition calls out those who claim to speak for Christ as false prophets and anti-Christs.

While most pro-Plump Christians prefer the *Cherry Picker's Version* of the Bible, the *King James Version offers* a host of citations about false prophets and false Messiahs.. For example, *Matthew 24:24 For there shall arise false Christs, and false prophets, and shall shew great signs and wonders; insomuch that, if (it were) possible the very elect.* Gulp! Heck, head to Seven-Eleven and make it a Big Gulp!

Would someone show that *Mark* reference to Reverend Pat?

Appendix B

Pagado por Mexico

In 2016, during his presidential campaign, Donald J. Plump said that he would build a wall on the Southern border between the United States and Mexico and that Mexico would pay for it. It was really a throwaway line but the audience reacted positively and every campaign stop after that Donny brought up the wall an asked a n excited crowd, "and who will pay for it?" And the audience should back "Mexico." The response was almost Pavlovian and you could see the Plumpanzees salivating as they shouted back "Mexico."

But Donny was never really serious. You see, folks, Donny never thought he would actually win. He really didn't want to win. He just wanted to enhance the Plump brand. That is what he promised Melania, that he would lose and that they would go back to playing a latter day version of Tom and Daisy Buchanan and return to Mar-a-Lago where the rich went to be rich together. Those were not tears of joy that escaped Melania's tear ducts on Election Night, those were tears of disappointment. A loss might have meant a cable channel or the very least a new show. Donny missed he limelight that *The Apprentice* provided. Donny was always the showman. And he had outdone himself, he had won the election. It wasn't that he was a wonderful candidate, far from it, but it seemed in three states which were normally Democratic (Pennsylvania, Michigan and Wisconsin) Donny squeaked by Mrs. Clinton by a total of 70,000votes out of several million cast. Only Hillary Clinton could not defeat Donny, she was the only Democrat who might lose and yes she won the popular vote by nearly three million votes, but the Electoral College went to Donny and that was that. I remember how shriveled up I became when Donny got the word that he won; he had no idea what to do. And he certainly was not thinking of building a wall on the Mexican border or getting the Mexicans to pay for it.

Funny thing is for the first two years of Donny's term the Republicans controlled not only the White House but the House and Senate as well. If the Mexicans were not going to pay for the wall, the Republicans had the votes to secure funding for the Wall. But they didn't give a shit. They wanted conservative judges and a big tax cut for their rich donors. Donny forgot about the Wall and the Democrats offered him a deal, DACA for the wall funding, but he rejected it. A year later the Democrats regained the House and the Wall was a dead issue.

But with 2020 on the horizon and an unfulfilled promise of the Wall looming over his campaign Donny decided to raid the Pentagon to build his wall.

By Executive Action, no less. Obsequious senators from states which housed military facilities that were targeted for cuts went meekly along with Donny rather than face his wrath and a subsequent primary opponent. A Red state senator fears no Democrat, only a Republican primary opponent. So they caved, as Donny knew they would. Even Moscow Mitch was silent while Fort Campbell Kentucky lost its middle school for the children of service members. You might sing a bit of Pink Floyd that Mitch and the others were "just another brick in the wall," and that they "don't need no education," at Fort Campbell.

On January 11, 2019, Donny denied that he ever said that Mexico would pay for the Wall…send the denial over to Winston Smith at the Ministry of Truth, we have gone full Orwellian.

Appendix C
Where's My Emmy?

Among Donny's most lingering resentments is the fact that he never won an Emmy. Never mind that Donny never won an Oscar or a Golden Globe, but it frosts his cake that *The Apprentice* never copped a statuette of a winged woman holding an outstretched atom above her head, which is called an Emmy.

Donny could, however, take home an Envy, a statue for which I guess the color would be green and it would be a statue of a little man holding up a middle finger to the world. If not winning an Emmy frosts Donny's cake the extra sprinkles which have been added to said cake are that Michelle and Barak Obama might win an Emmy for their Netflix program *American Factory,* heck maybe even an Academy Award for Best Documentary It is bad enough that Michelle's *Becoming* was a runaway best seller, but tee-vee? That is Donny's vast wasteland, to borrow Newt Minow's phrase. The Obamas' Higher Ground Productions signed a multi-year deal with Netflix a deal that might have been Donny's had he not won the damn election in 2016. It wasn't fair that ex-presidents can make gobs of money AFTER they leave office when it is so difficult to get a little sweetener out of the Pentagon to support failing resort properties in Ireland and Scotland or spend over a hundred mil on a little golf now or then, or promoting Doral as a location for the next G-7 meeting. As for as Donny is concerned the Emoluments Clause does not apply to him, anyway. And look at Jimmy Carter, how much does he skim off the top for those Habitat for Humanity Houses anyway? Nobody busts his ass for nothing, Donny says. What is Carter like 103? Making a buck off the office of president is just business. A Plump Tower in Moscow and two in Saudi Arabia. I mean it is difficult to keep the money laundering thing going when all of those *New York Times* reporters are always snooping around. Pesky little trolls. Can't launder more than a million or two a week for our Russian friends.

But no worries on the cash flow. Like so many things in Washington, the White House can be a gold mine of graft if done properly. I mean look at Moscow Mitch's net worth twenty-some million on a Senator's salary. You don't think Moscow Mitch didn't get a little kickback from the

Russian oligarch over that aluminum plant for Hillbillyland?

And, of course, if the American people ever actually see Donny's tax returns, game over. I will be limp for the rest of my days.

Appendix D
Nuking Hurricanes & Sharpiegate

I think the Weather Service made a mistake in naming their hurricanes in 2019. As you may know they select names alphabetically, the first storm of the season bearing an Alpha designation. The fourth storm of the Atlantic Hurricane Season received a Delta designation of Dorian, but I think Donald would have been more appropriate, considering what transpired. Instead we got Dorian and he was a doozy, a Category 5 hurricane, a category which Donny, a property owner in Florida, claimed he had never heard of. Well there was Andrew in 1992 and the Labor Day Hurricane in 1935. Those were Florida storms. Need I repeat that Donny is not well read. Category, smatagory…

Besides, Donny thought, we could just a nuke a hurricane anyway to prevent it from hitting Mar-a-Lago…ah I mean Florida, of course. Jonathan Swan from *Axios* reported Donny discussing nuking hurricanes with Homeland Security which led to a spate of tweets by Donny denying any such conversation. But like the boy who tweeted "wolf" Donny's denials only confirmed the conversation.

As Swan reported, Donny said, in his own version of a Eureka moment, “I got it. I got it. Why don’t we nuke them? They start forming off the coast of Africa, as they’re moving across the Atlantic, we drop a bomb inside of the hurricane and it disrupts it. Why can’t we do that?”

And so help me- for I was there- the guy who briefed the president somehow kept a straight face and replied, “Sir, we will look into that.”

Swan reported that the briefer was “knocked back on his heels. You could have heard a gnat fart in the meeting. People were astonished.” They sure were; I was there.

The National Oceanic and Atmospheric Administration (NOAA), which is in charge of weather predictions published a note about nuclear bombs and hurricanes which states,

“Apart from the fact that this might not even alter the storm, this approach neglects the problem that the released radioactive fallout would fairly quickly move with the trade winds to affect land areas and cause devastating environmental problems. Needless to say, this is not a good idea.”

So at least Donny didn’t nuke Dorian and give the Florida orange crop a really tangy flavor with a fatal aftertaste. No, Dorian smashed into the Bahamas after first being a threat to, as Donny tweeted, Alabama. Now Clemson is a threat to Alabama, that's for sure. They are every year, but Dorian wasn't. Forecasts be damned, Donny had tweeted Dorian was a threat to Alabama. And when the weather folks in Alabama tweeted that Alabama was not in the path of the hurricane, Hurricane Donald went Cat 5 in the White House. Someone had corrected the Donald. So NOAA, normally the good guys in the weather business found some black hats around the office, put them on and corrected, I kid you not, the weather folks in Birmingham for correcting President Plump. You see, they said, Alabama had been in the path of the storm and the president produced a weather map and with black *Sharpie* markings which added Alabama to the cone of uncertainty. Yup, the agency we count on for honest weather forecasts fudged one for the Donald. But hey, at least he didn't nuke Dorian, right?

And the poor Bahamians. They lost everything. Less than a hundred miles from the USA, our ally, our friendly neighbor. Surely we could let them come to Florida on a mission of mercy. If only they were white we might have.

Epilogue II
The Sequel

So now, Dear Reader it is your turn to take notes on the tenure of Donald J. Plump. The Donald has been called a "con man" which is short for "Confidence Man," a guy who gains your trust and confidence before he sells you some swamp land in the Everglades. Donny is a consummate Confidence Man who was genuinely surprised at the gullibility of the American people in 2016. Are you one of his believers?

I have left a blank page for each month of 2020. I will help you out with January, but then you are on your own. I am worn out. Will I ever stand up again? This is one Plump Tower that will never go up.

January 2020

Dumb stuff Donny said...

Dumb shit Donny did...

February 2920

March 2020

April 2020

May 2020

June 2020

July 2020

August 2020

September 2020

October 2020

November 2020 & Election Day

Made in the USA
Columbia, SC
30 September 2019